Ancient Mythology

Captivating Stories, Magic, Mystery & Legendary Myths of The World Throughout History Revealed

Table of Contents

Introduction

Stories run in our blood. Since the day we were born, we were raised by tales of the wonderful and strange - from the bedtime stories we were told in our years of infancy, to stories we live to tell our grandkids. When looked at from a broader perspective, these stories don't seem to matter much. But on a grander scale, they mean more than we can possibly imagine.

This book is dedicated to stories; the first stories ever told. The tales of heroes, gods, and kings all over the world. What they did, how they did it, and why they did it. Not only that, but you'll also get to go back in time and see how adults used to explain creation to their children, and how they made sense of all that was unknown to them.

In these next chapters, you'll be led in chronological order from the earliest epics of Ancient Sumer, through the mysterious lands of Egypt and China, until you reach the mighty Greeks. But it won't stop there. We'll also take a quick look at the most famous Aztec and Celtic mythologies, too.

So, get ready to immerse yourself into a primordial sea of culture, and a wonderful epic of story-telling like no other.

Chapter 1 - Monsters, Animals, and Demons

Before delving into the realm of stories and legends, here's a quick guide to any and all mythical creatures that you might stumble upon while reading this book. For ease of use, you'll find that they're arranged by their order of appearance.

Sumerian Mythology:

Humbaba

The Giant is featured in the Sumerian legend, The Epic of Gilgamesh, as the keeper of the Cedar Forest. He had a human body covered in scales, the head, and paws of a lion, and the claws of a vulture on his feet. Stories also mention that he had bull horns and that both his tail and penis were snakeheads. One of the high gods, Enlil had put him on the edge of the forest to protect it from humans, which he did, until he was killed by Gilgamesh and Enkidu.

Egyptian Mythology:

Scarab

One of the most significant insects in the history of ancient Egypt is the sacred scarab; which is a type of dung beetle. On some occasions, it was used as a protection spell or as part of an amulet to protect a mummy during its journey through the underworld. It was also believed that Kephri, a beetle-faced god, was responsible for rolling Ra (the Sun) across the sky each day.

Sphinx

Popular in Egyptian and Greek mythology, the sphinx is a creature with the body of a lion and the head of a human. The main differences between the two variations are that in Greece, the monster is often depicted as a woman, and it was of a malicious nature. On the other hand, the standard Egyptian sphinx had the head of a man while, on other occasions, it had the head of a pharaoh as a way of expressing divinity. As for its nature, the sphinx is portrayed as a good-natured creature unless faced with an enemy, in which case it becomes deadly. The mythical being was associated with protection and guardianship and usually placed around tombs.

Greek Mythology:

Cerberus

Despite the common misconception, hellhounds do not exist solely in Greek mythology. We see them mentioned in Welsh, Catalan, and Norse mythologies, too. Yet, the fact remains that Cerberus, the hound of Hades, is the most famous of all.

The Greek monster was an offspring of Echidna, a snake-woman and the mother of monsters, and Typhon, a giant multi-headed serpent-human-dragon hybrid who, at some point, waged war on the ancient Greek gods. He was a terrifyingly large three-headed black hound, with serpent heads for tails, who served Hades in the underworld. The hound was tasked with guarding the gates of Tartarus so that no one could go in or out.

The only times Cerberus was featured in stories was whenever anyone descended to the underworld. When it came to

Heracles' twelve labors, capturing Cerberus and delivering him to King Eurystheus was the final labor. And, as you'll see, the hellhound is not always impossible to beat.

The Hundred-handed Ones | Hecatoncheires

These three extremely powerful giants were the sons of Uranus, but they were imprisoned by him at birth. As the name suggests, they were said to have a hundred hands each, as well as fifty heads which, in addition to their strength, made them valuable allies in times of war. With the rule of the Titans, the hundred-handed ones remained in prison and were only freed by Zeus at the start of the Titanomachy (the Great War).

Before waging war on the Titans, Zeus went to speak to Gaia (Earth), the mother of all. She told him that the Olympians were destined to win the war, but only with the help of the Hecatoncheires. So, he went to free them and, in return, they fought by his side. After the war, they were assigned to guard the Titan prisoners in Tartarus.

Celtic Mythology:

Donn Cuailnge

In Celtic myths, he's known as the Brown Bull of Cooley who was the reason for the battle between Ulster and Queen Medb. Before turning into a bull, he was a pig shepherd who worked for the king of Munster. During a fight with another shepherd who worked for the province of Connacht, they both turned into worms. These worms were then swallowed by two cows. The result was that the two shepherds were reborn in the form of two bulls; one belonged to Dáire mac Fiachna, and one to

Queen Medb but eventually found his way into King Ailill's herd. Both bulls were extremely strong and fertile.

Chinese Mythology:

Qilin

It is a legendary Chinese creature with a large, dragon-like head and a body that's similar in shape to that of a horse or an ox. In addition, it is commonly depicted with a single horn, cloven hooves, and fish-like features such as scales and barbels. Despite their vicious appearance, they were said to be so gentle that they refused to set their hooves on grass so as not to harm a single blade. In ancient myths, like that of the Yellow Emperor, their sighting is regarded as a sign that a great and wise king would pass away, or that one would be born.

Kua Fu

He was a giant drought-demon who attempted to catch the sun. During his chase, he drank all the rivers and lakes and brought a drought upon the land. Some accounts say he was killed by dehydration. Others say, he was killed by the mighty winged dragon, Yinglong, which was a rain deity.

Chapter 2 - Natural Phenomena Inspiring Myths

We live on a rock that is suspended in space by invisible forces. While this sentence sounds a tad too magical, it is true. Perhaps modern science took the element of fantasy out of our lives, but for those in the past, fantasy was all they had. In the face of all-natural phenomena and peculiar happenings, Earth's earliest inhabitants had no choice but to resort to storytelling to make sense of the world.

Earthquakes

It's only human nature to find the meaning behind things that remain inexplicable to us; we reason our way through it, even if it sounds too far-fetched at times. And, the First Japanese were no different. They believed that Numazu, the bringer of chaos and destruction, shakes the Earth for a valid reason.

Japan has been prone to numerous Earthquakes over the years; seismologists justify this natural disaster by explaining that the Japanese archipelago lies where many oceanic plates intersect. However, the Ancient Japanese didn't have any means of justification that could explain why this phenomenon continued to occur almost ritually. And, so they built a story about a massive catfish monster; Namazu that lived beneath the Earth and spontaneously swam through the crashing waves of its entangled oceans and rivers, causing several Earthquakes.

Earthquakes weren't only an emblem of destruction; they were also viewed as bringers of good fortune to the poor. According to Japanese mythology; the gigantic monster was responsible for restoring the world on a regular basis; the phenomenon is known as the Yonasoshi. The lower class viewed every Earthquake as a chance for them to rise. Namazu doesn't only shake Japan's plates, but it also shakes the higher class and allows a balanced financial redistribution among the people.

Fire

Aside from volcanoes, fire doesn't naturally exist around us. That particular fact is all we need to explain why ancient civilizations thought it was not an Earthly object. Think about it. In order to have a fire, one needs to create it. But how did it come to be? That was the question civilizations hoped to answer, from the Greeks who believed a Titan stole fire from the gods and gave it to humanity, to the Vikings who believed that Loki bought the secrets of fire from an eagle. One culture, however, stands out with a captivating albeit lesser-known myth.

The Leni Lenape and the Legend of the Rainbow Crow

These were the Native American tribes who lived across the northeastern United States and Southern Canada. For them, fire came into this world long before man, when animals dominated the Earth.

Ever since its birth, the world was full of greenery and warmth. Until one day, the spirit of snow arrived. Kijiamuh Ka'ong, the Creator Who Creates By Thinking What Will Be, had thought of cold, and there it was, threatening animals, freezing waters, and wilting plants. It was then that the animals thought it would be best to convene and try to come up with a solution before the world froze over.

The owl, being the wisest of creatures, explained that there was only one way. One of them had to take on the task of flying up to the heavens where the Creator dwelled, and ask him to think of warmth as he once did. However, as wise as it was, the owl knew its vision wouldn't allow it to get so close to the sun. So, the job would have to fall to someone else, both fast and clever, who had to make the journey.

Time passed, and several animals volunteered; a turtle, a coyote, and others, of which none was suitable for the mission. Meanwhile, the snow grew deeper, and the animals grew more anxious. That was when they heard a sound sweeter than anything they had ever heard; it was enough to distract them from all their troubles momentarily. It was the Rainbow Crow, with feathers of utmost beauty and the most vivid colors. It told everyone it would fly to the heavens without falter, and convince the creator to bring back warmth.

As the animals on Earth rejoiced and sang for the crow, it took flight. Three days later, the crow stood before the Creator, who was rather busy to notice the bird. Rainbow Crow started singing, hoping to get the Creator's attention. The song captivated Kijiamuh Ka'ong so much that he decided to grant Rainbow Crow one gift in return.

The crow immediately asked for the snow to stop, but the Creator explained that he couldn't, "for the snow has a spirit of its own." Even if he stopped it, the Earth would still be cold. In place, Kijiamuh Ka'ong offered him the gift of fire to preserve the warmth and melt the snow. He poked at the sun with a stick, then handed the stick to Rainbow Crow and commanded him to bring it down to Earth before it died out.

Onwards flew the crow until he brought fire to Earth. But by the time he had reached the ground, the fire had taken its toll on him. His feathers and beak were burnt and blackened, and his voice was hoarse and gravely from the smoke. Yet, he was still celebrated among all the animals, and the Native Americans to come.

Hot Springs and Seismic Activities

The Oracle of Delphi is a huge part of Greek Mythology. She was an oracle often consulted by anyone who could afford to pay her before embarking on a great endeavor. She was even believed to have predicted the Trojan war.

Legends say that the oracle first belonged to the Earth and was guarded by a dragon. When Apollo first set foot on Delphi, he slew the dragon and claimed the oracle to himself, using her to voice his prophecies. When people came to Apollo's temple seeking counsel, the oracle would enter the shrine and sit on a chair, then inhale a vapor that erupted from a crevice in the ground. The gasses sent her into a trance-like state, which allowed her to speak in tongues that the priests would then interpret to people.

Ages later, geologists and archaeologists determined that the temple was built above multiple planar fractures, as well as a hot spring, and a bituminous limestone formation. This meant that the vapors released from the spring passed through the hydrocarbon gases trapped in the limestone formation. The end product of the reaction was a gas with narcotic effects. In other words, the one speaking through the oracle was none other than narcotic vapors that erupted from the ground.

Eclipses

The eclipse is one of those seemingly magical phenomena. It's when the sun and moon meet and create a mystic effect in the sky that we are advised not to look at directly. And, even though we now understand what causes the Eclipse, the people of Benin didn't.

All the way in West Africa, Benin was known to be the home of the Dahomey Kingdom. This kingdom flourished in the 16th century and continued to grow until it reached its end in the 18th Century. The Fon people were proud of their Dahomean beliefs; they openly celebrated their goddess; Nana Buluku, and religiously awaited the blessings that she would bequeath onto them. Nana Buluku, the supreme creator, had twins; Mawu and Lisa. Mawu was the goddess of the moon, while Lisa was the god of the sun.

Mawu was the source of wisdom and intellect; she was a motherhood figure, who was associated with joy, moon, and cool nights. She created life in all its forms. She even attempted to save the planet from chaos more than once. According to this Ancient African mythology, Mawu witnessed disorder and confusion taking place on Earth, so she sent Lisa to invent tools and teach men how to use them, so they can create farms and live a civilized life.

Another time, the moon goddess was gazing down at Earth and admiring the life that she had created there. But, the more she gazed, the more she realized that the planet might be too heavy now and that its inhabitants might be in real danger. Filled with concern, Mawu called upon the Ancient Serpent, Ayida-Weddo, to circle the bottom of the Earth and thrust it into space with its body.

Even though there are stories that don't have Mawu and Lisa in the same place, Ancient Africans depicted the celestial couple as one. They often referred to them as Mawu, and they were viewed as an androgynous spirit. This duality was shown in many ways in this mythology, and one of them was the Eclipse. Whenever the natives witnessed an eclipse, they would know it as a sign of lovemaking between Mawu and Lisa.

Rainbows

Of all the inventions that mankind has developed over the years, stories remain the one thing that does not need much to create. They helped people go about their day, make sense of the world, and were the fastest to spread. In fact, the Aboriginals, Natives of Australia, had a lot in common with the Dahomean mythology. One of the most significant creatures they shared with each other is the Rainbow Snake; also known as the Ayida-Weddo.

The Aboriginals believed that the Rainbow Serpent was a divine being that roamed in a timeless space called "the dreaming." It traveled around the world through waterholes, and it's said that when it does so, a rainbow appears in the sky. So, imagine the aboriginal's excitement when they saw their creator traveling through their sky and could witness him moving his multi-colored skin above them.

To Native Australians, the Rainbow Serpent was the creator of all life on Earth and beyond. It is normally associated with rainbows, fertility, and water. However, when angered by mischievous people who ignore the rules, it becomes associated with thunder, storms, and floods. It's said that this majestic being leaves spirit-children in different water holes so that women can be impregnated if they stay in the water long enough.

Floods

The ancient Egyptians' lives were always eventful. Some were training to be scribes, while others were scribes in training to become doctors. Some were busy with casting spells and offering prayers and good omens to the people, while others were tasked with farming and taking care of the animals. Even though they all had different tasks, their lives revolved around one thing; the annual flood of the Nile.

Imagine an overflow of water that can cover an entire city; it's nothing short of terrifying. However, ancient Egyptians didn't await this seasonal event with fear in their hearts. They regarded it as a blessing from the Nile god, Hapi. Their whole year circulated around this particular event; they could never know whether there would be an overwhelming, insignificant, or just the right amount of flood, which is why the mythology speaks of an annual celebration to appease Hapi, by throwing the most beautiful virgin maiden into the water. They called her "The bride of the Nile."

The Nile worshippers would carry her on a chariot and celebrate her holy wedding day, where she would meet her husband, Hapi, in another life. The Nile bride would have both arms chained to her sides, and she would happily throw herself into the Nile.

This ritual guaranteed the ancient Egyptians that Hapi wouldn't drown their land or give them too little water; he would bless them with the right amount of flow because they had given him a new bride to bless him with offspring.

Chapter 3 - Sumerian Myths and Gods

About 3,000 years before the birth of Christ, the Sumerians reigned as the earliest civilization on Earth, which is why their legends and deities are, by far, one of the greatest creative achievements. As you're reading, keep in mind that the authors and poets had almost no influence other than the nature around them.

The Sumerian Pantheon

As with the study of any civilization's mythology, it's best to start with an approach that takes the main deities and their origins into consideration. For the Sumerians, the assembly of the gods was hierarchical, since each god served a purpose when it came to rule over the universe. Ruling over all was An, God of Heaven.

Second to An were Enlil, the executor of the gods' will, and the god of the wind and agriculture. At the time, people thought of the warm gusts of wind as Enlil's breath, which was often interpreted as his will or command. Third of the main four was Enki, whose wit and resourcefulness was often put to use. After creating man, he formed a bond with the creature and is seen to come to its aid throughout several myths. He was also loved by both mortals and gods, which paved the way for him to go against all gods and save mankind from the Great Flood. Last was the mother of all life, Ninhursag. In many myths, she plays the role of a creator, or more accurately, a birther of life.

Followed by the divine four came three more gods to form the seven who "decree the fates." Utu, the sun god, was responsible for justice, overseeing all that lies under the sun and protecting mortals. Nanna, the moon god, who emerged from the nether world every night, and went back each morning to resume his duties of issuing a judgment on the dead. And finally, Inanna, the most famous female deity in Sumerian mythology whose myths mostly revolve around her attempts to overthrow the rule of other deities. She represented love, sexuality, and war.

Scripts mention a large number of other great gods, yet none were higher in rank than the "seven who decree."

The Creation of Man

Some say it was the coming of the female deities, or the refusal of the younger gods to play their part in running the universe, that caused the world to reach a state of imbalance. The Annunaki, the high gods, started complaining as they had no one to maintain the world. As the gods looked to Enki for help because of his wisdom, he was too deep in slumber that he couldn't hear them at all. That was when his mother, Nammu, the birth giver of the great gods, came up with the idea of creating creatures to do the bidding of her sons.

Nammu then went and awakened Enki from his sleep, and told him of what was happening, and of her wish to create loyal servants for the gods. He agreed to make them and told her to fashion them in the likeness of the gods out of clay. Enki also said that Ninhursag, the goddess of birth, was going to be of Nammu's aid as she shaped mankind.

Man, as Enki called his creature, was to be bound to the mold of the gods by Ninhursag to guarantee perfection. Man's purpose was to serve the gods, and when the time came for them to die, their souls would descend to the netherworld (the underworld) where they would be judged by the sun god, Utu, and have their fates decided by the moon-god, Nanna.

The Great Flood

According to a poem found inscribed on a broken chunk of a clay tablet at Nippur, Iraq, after the creation of man, cities, and kingships, the Sumerian gods decreed that the Earth was to be destroyed by a flood. However, it was not a unanimous decision. Enki, who was believed to be the god of the subterranean freshwater ocean and the son of An (the supreme creator), decided to rebel by helping the humans survive the flood.

For that reason, Enki went to Ziusudra, a king and a priest, and told him what the gods An and Enlil, were going to do. Then, Enki instructed Ziusudra to build a large boat and stock it with pairs of animals. When it was time, "All the evil winds, all stormy winds gathered into one and with them, them, the Flood was sweeping over (the cities of) the half-bushel baskets, for seven days and seven nights."

The world was taken over by that flood, but Ziusudra and everyone inside the boat remained safe. On the eighth day, the sun-filled the sky and the water had retreated. That's when Ziusudra left his boat and, looking unto Utu, the sun god; he started sacrificing oxen and sheep as a sign of gratitude.

When Enlil found that not all mankind was erased, his anger broiled, which led Enki to justify what he had done to protect the human race. Ziusudra was then brought before the gods, An and Enlil, and he was blessed with eternal life because of his obedience and servitude to the gods. "And Enlil did well by him, granting him life like a god's, making the lasting breath of life like gods descend into him." Not only that, but the gods also made him ruler and protector over all small animals, as well as, the son of man.

The Epic of Gilgamesh

The first literary work of this nature known to man, The Epic of Gilgamesh, has been documented in Sumerian and Akkadian. Because of the slight differences in cultures, the two versions also happen to contain small differences, yet the main storyline is the same.

Gilgamesh was one of the mightiest kings of the land of Uruk. His might, though, came only from his status as a demi-god and his supernatural physical abilities. As a king, he was not fair. He ruled with terror, enslaved his own people, and took what he pleased. Whoever stood in his way, faced Gilgamesh's wrath. The people of Uruk cried out to the gods, time and again, until they finally answered.

The supreme god, An, heard. He created a twin for Gilgamesh of equal strength so that he may fight the tyrant and rid the people from his rule. Enkidu, the twin, was sent down to Uruk where he was found by a young trapper in the wilderness next to a watering hole. When the trapper saw the wild Enkidu, he became frightened and ran to his father, who sent him to Gilgamesh. Upon hearing the boy's story, he sent Shamhat, a sacred prostitute, back with the trapper. The king's orders were for Shamhat to expose herself and reveal her sexuality to him.

The trapper took Shamhat to the watering hole, where she took off her clothes. Enkidu was drawn to her, and they had sex for six days and seven nights until he was satisfied. As he turned back to the wilderness, his body wasn't capable of running as fast as the animals around him. He found his understanding had changed. With Shamhat's help, he had become more civilized. Then, the harlot took him to see Gilgamesh.

In the streets of Uruk, the two fought. Gilgamesh won the fight, but he didn't kill Enkidu. Instead, he was captivated by the man's strength above all men, so he decided they should be allies. While talking, Enkidu mentioned a horrendous monster, Humbaba the Terrible, with a lion head and a mighty roar that shook mountains. He said that the monster, beloved by the gods, was appointed by Enlil, a guardian to the Cedar Forest, to terrorize humans and that no human was able to set foot in the giant's dominion.

Craving the challenge, Gilgamesh set out to glorify his own name, and with him, he took Enkidu. Standing on the edge of the forest, they could see the track marks made by Humbaba. So, Gilgamesh prayed to Utu for help. When Humbaba came out to face them, he was trapped and blinded by thirteen winds which gave Gilgamesh and Enkidu the advantage.

Humbaba was slain by the two heroes, and they cut the forest cedars, made a raft and sailed to Nippur, where Enlil was, to boast and bring him the head of his beloved giant. Then, they returned to Uruk to celebrate. After a long journey, Gilgamesh was cleaning himself when Inanna, appeared to him. She tried to seduce him, but he rejected her because she was known to bring destruction to all her lovers.

The goddess of love, war, and sexuality did not take to the mortal's rejection. She went to her father, An, and threatened to break down the doors of the underworld and unleash the dead on the living if she was not given the bull of heaven. Wanting to avoid chaos on his creation, An granted her the bull. Without faltering, Inanna sent the beast down to Uruk to kill Gilgamesh, but instead, he killed it with Enkidu's help. Not only that, but Enkidu also humiliated Inanna in the process by cutting out the bull's thigh and flinging it at her.

The gods viewed the killing of the bull and the humiliation of Inanna as the last straw. They decided they wouldn't spare the men any longer. In his sleep, Gilgamesh saw the gods together. They were discussing what to do with Gilgamesh and Enkidu. Finally, they arrived at the decision that they should kill Enkidu. Terrified by the dream, Gilgamesh went to awaken his friend, but Enkidu's heart had stopped.

Confronted with the corpse of his identical twin, Gilgamesh realized his own mortality, and the once fearless warrior became overwhelmed by a fear of death. The only solution that came to his mind was acquiring immortality. Gilgamesh mourned his friend, gathered his courage, and ventured out to the land behind the mountain range where no human was allowed. He went to seek the secrets of immortality from Ziusudra (Utnapishtim in Akkadian) who ruled over Dilmun.

When he arrived at Mount Mashu, the entrance to where Ziusudra lived, Gilgamesh found the gates guarded by scorpion-men. After convincing them to let him in, he traveled 12 leagues in complete darkness until he came out the other side. Among the cedar and the blue sea and the other marvels of the land behind the mountain, he spotted a tavern. Siduri, the tavern-keeper, had bolted its doors shut in fear of Gilgamesh, but she told him that he should go to Urshanabi, a ferryman that would give him passage across the Waters of Death to where Ziusudra lived.

Gilgamesh did as he was told, and he met with Ziusudra. First, Ziusudra tried to explain that the gods were restless and sleepless and that immortality was not glamorous, but Gilgamesh's heart was set. So, after telling Gilgamesh of the great flood and how Ziusudra had received immortality himself, he presented the man with a challenge; if he could stay awake for a week, he would be given immortality. Overcome with exhaustion from his journey, Gilgamesh failed. After pleading for a second chance, Ziusudra told Gilgamesh of a plant at the bottom of the sea that had the ability to make him younger.

Excited and relieved, Gilgamesh tied himself to heavy rocks; they dragged him down to the bottom of the sea where he managed to capture the plant. On his way back to Uruk, he stopped to bathe, and that was when a snake caught the flower's scent and snatched it away. Disappointed beyond belief, Gilgamesh returned to Uruk. But, as he gazed upon the great walls of his city, he realized that his deeds would be immortalized in the glorious city he had built for his people.

Inanna's Descent to the Netherworld

Inanna was the queen of heaven, a goddess of great ambition. When she set her heart on going to the netherworld, her duties didn't stand in her way. Her sole goal was to overthrow the rule of her older sister, Ereshkigal, and take the land of the dead for herself. For that, she left her duties and post and started on the journey from heaven to Earth and below, but not before she took precautions.

She knew the difficulty of the feat she was about to attempt, so she gave her minister, Ninšubur, orders on what to do in the event of her death. When she arrived at the gates of the underworld, he was to make laments for her, mourn her among the gods, and pray for their protection over her. Then, Ninšubur was to appeal to Enlil, first, to restore her to life. If he refused to help, the minister was to go to Nanna. If he also refused to help, he was to go to Enki, for his wisdom knew no bounds.

Inanna made sure to dress in beauty for the journey. A pala dress that signified her femininity, a turban, twin egg-shaped beads on her breasts, and a golden ring on her finger. She also took great care in expressing her divine attributes, her *me*, using her clothing. She wore a beaded necklace and held a measuring rod and a measuring tape, all made of the treasurable lapis-lazuli stone. It was to resemble her beauty, wisdom, and power.

At the first gate, she found herself facing the chief keeper of the netherworld's doors, Neti, whom she told she had come to pay respects for her sister's dead husband. When Ereshkigal got news of Inanna's visit, she commanded that the seven gates of the underworld be locked, and opened one by one as Inanna was gradually stripped of her clothing. Just as one couldn't ascend to Earth after descending into the netherworld, one also couldn't be granted passage inside unless naked.

After passing the seventh door, Inanna was brought to kneel before her sister's throne in front of all seven of the underworld's judges, the Annunaki. When she attempted to overtake the throne, they struck her with the "look of death," spoke her fate, and instantly, she was dead. It is said that her defeat was due to each of her powers, leaving her with each piece of garment that was stripped away.

Innana's corpse was hung on a stake in the underworld for three full days. Meanwhile, Ninšubur's concern grew for his goddess, but as instructed, he went to Enlil's temple to plead for help. Enlil took no action because he saw that it was Inanna's own arrogance and greed that led to her demise. As for Nanna, he refused to help and replied with the same answer. Enki, however, took pity on her soul and set out to restore her.

Enki knew about the life-giving plant and the life-giving water. If both were applied on Inanna, she would be restored, but he needed someone to fetch her corpse. For that, he created two creatures out of dirt, kur-jara, and gala-tura. He then gave one the plant and the other the water and commanded them to go to the netherworld. The creatures were ordered to slip past the guards and the seven doors, offer sympathy to the queen whom they would find agonizing, and in exchange, ask for nothing but Inanna's body. After that, they had to apply the plant and the water on her corpse to bring her back.

And so, the creatures did as they were told and Inanna rose from the dead. As she was making her way out of the underworld, she was seized by the Anunnaki. "Who has ever ascended from the underworld, has ascended unscathed from the underworld? If Inanna is to ascend from the underworld, let her provide a substitute for herself," they said, according to the myth. It was another rule governing the realm of the dead which the goddess was forced to obey. She left the underworld escorted by armed demons big and small to find her substitute.

On her journey back, Inanna was met by her loyal servant Ninšubur, who was about to be captured by the demon horde when the goddess stopped them. She wouldn't let them take her servant, who had stayed true to her words. Nor did she let the demons take Shara and Latarak, the patron-gods of Umma and Bad-tibira, because she saw that they had dutifully mourned her passing. However, by the end of her journey, she passed by the city over which her husband, Dumuzi, ruled. She found that he was sitting on his throne, clothed in his royal attire, while she faced the terror of the underworld.

With that, she wasn't pleased. Anger coursed through her veins, and she shouted for the demons to take him back to their mistress. Without wait, the blood-thirsty demons carried the wailing, crying god back to the netherworld as Inanna's replacement.

Sumerian Mythology influenced others

As much as it is painful to abandon one great civilization and go to the next, we can't help but be in awe at how influential these seemingly trivial and outlandish stories were, and still are. Generations passed these stories on, each adding their own touches until the myths found their way, somehow, to our modern times.

Chapter 4 - Egyptian Gods, Goddesses, and Pharaohs

The Order of the World

Long before Ancient Egypt flourished into the great empire we all know, it was only but a few independent city-states that resided next to the Nile. Historians claim that it took several years for Egypt's lower and upper kingdoms to finally unite. And this union didn't only bring together lands. It also united people's faiths, habits, and ways of life. But, if this were the case, then how did people perceive the world before the unification?

The mythology of Ancient Egypt's creation takes place in four different states. Heliopolis, Memphis, Elephantine, and Hermopolis. And, every state had its own myth.

The people of Heliopolis, who resided in Lower Egypt, believed that there was nothing on Earth except the waters of Nun, the god of primeval water. And when the time was right, Atum, arose from the eternal depth of Nun's water. Atum became the ultimate creator of everything that came to be. He solely created Shu, the air, and Tefnut, the light. Together, they lived upon the waves of Nun, until his two children separated and left Atum alone. He loved his children deeply, which made him rejoice and cry in happiness when he saw them again. His tears gave birth to all mankind, which forced the god of the gods and his children to create a world where human beings could live.

Much like Heliopolis' myth of creation, the people of Memphis believed that there was nothing but Nun's waters that covered the land. Atum came from Nun's heart and tongue, which lead to the creation of the nine famous gods; Shu, Tefnut, Geb, Nut, Osiris, Isis, Set, Nepthys, and Horus. But, because Nun was the initial of all these mighty gods, he was regarded as the greatest of all, which is why he created everything and built and designed Egypt from nothingness.

Elphantine's natives had a different story, though. According to mythology, Khnum existed beyond the dimensions of time. He created the first nine gods and built a celestial egg that the Sun God, or Rā, came from. Then began the creation of Earth; he made animals, plants, water, and everything else that inhabited it. Human beings were created by taking clay and structuring it on his potter's wheel. After that, he taught a man how to make different things and trade with other people from different lands.

The most interesting creation stories come from Hermopolis because this city doesn't have one story; it has two. One part of the mythology explains that before anything came to exist, there were the four gods with their counterparts. There were Nun and Nunnet, who were water. Heh and Hehet, who represented infinity. Kek and Keket, who were darkness. And finally, Amun and Amunet, who together were air. Together they came from nothingness and created the world. They created the Nile, which was regarded as one of their most significant creations because the Nile grew a lotus, which released a scarab beetle. The scarab turned itself into a celestial child, who the people came to know as Rā; or the sun. Rā then created mankind from his tears, and from his mouth, he created the rest of the gods.

Another story from Hermopolis features a cosmic egg that came from a primeval Ibis. This Ibis was the god Thoth, and from his egg came the god, Rā, which is why he is always depicted as half human and half bird. The sun god began creation and gave life to all the gods and mankind.

Book of the Dead

One of the fascinating facts about this book is that it is not only one book. On the contrary, it takes many forms, and they are all slightly different from one another. According to Egyptian Mythology, the underworld is a series of challenges that the spirit must be prepared for, or it would suffer in an endless void for eternity. But, unfortunately, only Pharaohs and the elite could afford their own manuscripts, which is why they often hired different scribes to customize their own version of the book of the dead based on the lives they led. It was only later in the New Kingdom that the pharaoh allowed everyone to have a book of the dead. This is specifically why, today, we have many versions of the same book.

One of many manuscripts of the book of the dead was fashioned by a scribe in Thebes named Ani. Ani lived a prosperous life in the New Kingdom era. However, he wasn't concerned with worldly riches as much as he was worried about the afterlife. Ani began losing people from his family, and he was terrified that they died without enough preparations for the underworld. Filled with distress, he decided to write a guide for surviving the underworld. And, this guide became known as The Papyrus of Ani.

It all begins with Ani's mummification. The priests remove all his organs and keep his heart, they wrap the body in linen, and they protect it with several incantations. They place a scarab amulet on Ani's heart so that he can later use it in the underworld. And, finally, they bury the book of the dead with him, so that he can go to heaven safely. Ani's soul leaves the physical realm and begins its journey by facing terrifying monsters who are waiting to devour him. His soul has to pass through twelve gates; these gates are guarded by hungry demons, vile creatures, deadly crocodiles, venomous snakes that breathe fire, and terrifying monsters. Apep, the serpent god of destruction, roams one of the darkest gates and devours the souls of the dead if they don't chant the name of the guardians and protectors. The only way Ani can survive the twelve chambers is if he uses the sixty-five magic spells and prayers written in the book of the dead, along with weapons and magical amulets that were left for him in his tomb.

Ani's soul successfully passes through the twelve gates, and it arrives at the Kingdom of the god of the underworld, Osiris. Within this kingdom, Ani's spirit enters the Hall of Truth where it meets Ma'at, the goddess of truth, harmony, balance, and justice. In this hall, Ani meets forty-two gods. He addresses each by name and confesses to each of them one sin that he has not committed. This is where the scarab on the heart comes into play. If the soul claims that it didn't pollute the Nile, but it did, the scarab protects the heart from remembering any memory that might endanger the soul. On his way to the forty-two gods, Ani also has to address the floor of the Hall of Truth, for it will test him and see if he is pure. After Ani successfully addresses the forty-two gods and they accept him, he is sent to his final destination. Ani is sent to Anubis, the god of the dead. Ani witnesses a large golden scale on which his heart has to prove that it is lighter than a feather, or else the giant monster Ammit, which is part leopard, crocodile, and hippopotamus, will devour him. If the scale shows that Ani's heart is pure, Rā takes Ani's spirit to Osiris, so he can send it to heaven.

The Ancient Ones and Mysticism

According to this ancient mythology, magic is far older than creation. Like Nun, it existed before everything else. In the Old Kingdom, the natives embodied the element of magic in a god who goes by the name of Heka, which is why they referred to magic itself as Heka. But, this particular god didn't have a temple of his own, and people didn't constantly pray to him because Heka wasn't like any god. This ancient god was in everything that the ancient Egyptians did; they always channeled his powers with medications, fertility, protection, etc. To him, this was a form of worship. However, he still required more direct attention, which he asked from all the selected priests and no one else.

Priests belonged in the high hierarchy in society. They were experts in practicing magic, reading complex ancient books, and performing menacing rituals. They were viewed as the guardians of Egypt, Pharaoh, and the people. They supposedly had sacred knowledge that the gods had bestowed onto them because they were the only ones who could fathom it with all its complexities.

However, that doesn't mean that magic was only accessible to priests. Doctors used it, as well, since Heka was also the god of medicine, and disease was considered to be supernatural. So, you can see why doctors used magic on their patients to cure them. Of course, medications weren't arbitrary, and they weren't mere spells. Doctors had had real medicines for the ill, but it was always accompanied by a healing spell, too.

As for regular people, magic was also well-incorporated into their daily lives. Of course, they weren't conducting any complex rituals or casting any dangerous spells, but they only used magical amulets to protect themselves and sometimes cast their own simple spells when priests weren't available. Natives would perform simple rituals to protect their household. They would also use charms to increase luck and fertility, improve their businesses, and ease any form of pain. But, they still resorted to seers, so they could look into their future and analyze their dreams, went to doctors, and had a priest cast a spell if needs for one arose.

There is a significant part of the Egyptian mythology that's devoted to magic and practitioners of all kinds. The engraved writings on the ancient walls describe holy, metallic wands that were only carried by magicians who summoned mighty deities and made them obey. It also describes chanting and loud music that people used to cast out evil spirits that caused harm. It's impossible to know whether the Ancient's magic was real or not, but even if it wasn't, at least they saw the world through a more wondrous lens.

Chapter 5 - Chinese Mythology

The First Living Being

Like all mythologies, the Chinese describe the time before creation as that dominated by chaos. However, it is what happens from there that's captivating. According to legends, one myth of creation states that chaos folded upon itself, compressing further and further until it became a cosmic egg. Inside the egg, the chaos separated into two opposing forces; Yin and Yang. The offspring of this balance in forces was a primitive human giant known as P'an Ku.

P'an Ku was a hairy giant clothed in fur. In addition to his humanoid features, he had two horns on the top of his head. After his emergence, P'an Ku used a tool (it is argued whether it was an ax or a chisel) to break the cosmic egg, and separate Yin from Yang. Then, upon separation, Yang formed the sky above, and Yin became the Earth below, and both were kept apart by P'an Ku.

As he propped up the sky, P'an Ku grew in size with each passing day, raising the sky up higher and higher above the Earth, until the giant was fully grown. By then, 18,000 years had passed, and the giant had reached the end of his life, the entirety of it spent in shaping the universe. When he died, his body decomposed, uniting him with his creation.

By his breath, the four winds and the clouds came to be. His left eye rose high, taking its place as the sun, and his right eye became the moon. His muscles, head, and limbs turned into land, mountains, and the four quarters of the world. His blood settled into cracks and crevices and formed the Earth's seas and rivers.

His beard floated above and scattered in the sky to form our familiar constellations. P'an Ku's sweat fell down from the sky as rain unto the forests, trees, and plants that were his hair and fur. The giant's bones and teeth sank into the Earth and turned into minerals and metals, and his marrow morphed into precious stones. Humans, then, came to exist when the winds carried away the fleas and mites that once had lived on his body, and sent them to Earth.

Nevertheless, this is only one account of how the world was created. Due to the size of China, there has been a vast number of myths and stories that explained the origins of the cosmos. From pillars holding up the skies, and a square Earth, to the belief that unity preceded everything, the Chinese mythology, with all its variations, is living proof of our limitless imagination and creativity, as a species.

The Yellow Emperor

According to some accounts, Huang Di, also known as the Yellow Emperor, is thought to be the father, or ancestor, of all the Chinese. Some myths depict him having four faces, while others have him playing the role of the God of thunder. However, one thing we know for sure is that he's one of the most famous characters in Chinese mythology.

Wuxing, a traditional Chinese philosophy, revolves around the belief that the world is made of five phases or states, and elements. One depiction of the Chinese pantheon explained that the world was divided into north, south, east, west, and center. Each region was a kingdom of its own and was appointed to a god or a ruler. In addition, each god controlled a specific element and a season of the year. Huang Di ruled over the central region, which gave him immeasurable power and control over the four remaining kingdoms, and elements.

Legends tell that Huang Di, despite having great power, was not one for war. He loved his people and made sure he kept the peace. Unfortunately, the other gods didn't share the same views. They decided to come together and conspire against the Yellow Emperor, who decided not only to fight back but also lead the army in battle himself.

One of the four gods was Yan Di, Huang Di's twin brother. Yet, their relationship did not stop them from fighting against each other. While the war was not as bloody as the one Huang Di fought with Chi You, it is said that streams of blood flowed across the battlefield. Another story talks about how Huang Di was aided by groups of animals; tigers, panthers, black bears, and phoenixes. Regardless of the myth's variations, they all end with the Yellow Emperor victorious.

Battle of Zhuolu

This was a legendary battle that took place in Zholou. It started off as a result of Chi You launching an attack over Huang Di's dominion. While Chi You was a descendant of Yan Di, he possessed a number of non-human features. Legends portray him as a man with six arms, four eyes, bull horns and a bronze head with a forehead made of metal. He was also believed to have powers, some accounts mentioning that he had a good command of weather control spells, which he used in the battle.

Chi You first came into battle extremely prepared, and that led to numerous casualties in the Huang Di's ranks. The beast led over seventy-two tribes and outnumbered the Yellow Emperor's soldiers two to one. That was in addition to Chi You's tribes being highly skilled at making weaponry, and they were known to be fearsome warriors. In the first battles, Chi You took Huang Di's forces by surprise when he sent in his warriors wrapped in a thick blanket of fog. Unable to find their way, Huang Di's forces were quickly subdued.

Huang Di, nevertheless, was a man of inventions. Before going into battle again, he had designed a chariot called the south-pointing chariot. It was similar to a wheelbarrow in shape and quite small in size. On top of it was a figure pointing southwards, and it was set to keep pointing there regardless of the chariot's direction. It was supposed to help the soldiers find their way through the fog.

During the battle, Huang Di used the aid of Yinglong, an ancient winged Dragon. The dragon, having power over rain, decided to store all of heaven's water and flood Chi You and his army. But, Chi You had allies of his own. He appealed to the Wind-God Feng Bo, Master of the Wind, and Yu Shi, Lord of Rain. Together, they unleashed a raging storm to empty Yinglong's reserves. That was when another deity, Ba, the Goddess of Droughts and Huang Di's daughter, came down from the heavens.

With her descent, the waters dried up instantly. She then turned to Chi You and along with Huang di, helped capture and murder him. Some accounts say that his limbs were severed and scattered all over China. Others say that, after the battle, Ba was cursed and bound to Earth where she lives in a rainless place. As for Huang Di, he reigned as an all-powerful emperor and lived to witness the appearance of a qilin before his death.

The Legend of the Immortal Snake

Amidst all the fascinating legends that have enriched China's folklore, one story stands out the most. And, even though there are several variations of it, the story still follows the unconditional love story of Xu Xian and Bai Suzhen.

Our story begins with a young herbalist named Xu Xian, who had left his job to open his own medicine shop. His master wasn't happy for him, and out of resentment had sold him rotten herbs as new inventory. But, Xu Xian only discovered his former boss' betrayal upon the arrival of his plague-stricken patients. He couldn't cure them with these foul herbs, but his wife, Bai Suzhen, had another idea. She took the herbs and made a special recipe that immediately cured his patients. Many ill civilians started flooding Xu Xian's shop, and one of them was his former boss. Word traveled fast, and the whole town knew about Bai Suzhen's recipe.

All was going well for the couple, until one day a monk, Fahai, approached Xu Xian and informed him that his wife was a demon. Xu Xian immediately dismissed the monk's ridiculous accusation, but the monk was restless. Fahai instructed Xu Xian to give a special wine to his wife on the fifth day of the fifth month, where demons are at their weakest. The young herbalist took the wine with no intent of using it. But the more the day approached, the more Xu Xian felt inclined to give it to his wife.

Once the wine touched Bai Suzhen's lips, she felt ill and ran to her bedroom. Out of concern, Xu Xian prepared a medicine for her, but to his surprise, his wife had turned into a giant white snake. Xu Xian collapsed on the floor and died from shock. It was only until Bai Suzhen had regained her powers that she tried to help her husband. However, she wasn't powerful enough to bring him back to life.

And, so Bai Suzhen began her journey to the longest mountain in Asia, the Kunlun Mountains. She traveled to the mountain on a cloud; it was the only way she could fetch the immortal herb that could revive him. However, this herb was heavily guarded by supernatural beings and a wise old man on top of the forbidden apex of the mountain. She transformed into a monk upon her arrival and fooled the mighty servants temporarily. As Bai Suzhen was trying to run away, the servants caught her. She coughed up a magic ball and attacked one of the servants, but her efforts weren't enough, and another servant caught her. She placed the herb under her tongue, which transformed both of them into their true enchanted forms. The powerful crane servant took advantage of the transformation and tried to choke her scaled body with his beak. Luckily, the servant stopped once the wise one appeared. The guardian was perplexed and asked her to explain herself. Why would she need an enchanted herb when she had powers? Bai Suzhen had no choice but to tell the old man her story.

Apparently, thousands of years ago, Bai Suzhen was still a small snake, and a homeless man was about to murder her. But, Xu Xian in this past life, saved young Bai Suzhen from her ill-fate. Bai Suzian fell in love with him and felt eternally grateful for his kindness.

The old guardian was touched by the story, and he let Bai Suzhen go, so she can save her husband. She floated back on a cloud on her way home and quickly placed the herb in her husband's mouth. Xu Xian gradually awakened and was relieved to see his wife back, for he loved her dearly.

Chapter 6 - The Major Figures of Greek Mythology

Birth of the Gods

Nearly all mythologies begin the same way, and Greek mythology is no different. This Ancient mythology starts with chaos dominating the universe; it was so dull and vast that Gaia, mother Earth, and her brother Tartarus had magically sprung out of the void. She was so fertile that she didn't need a partner to mate with; alone, she gave birth to Uranus, Pontus, and Ourea. Together, they were the primordial sky, ocean, and mountains.

The cycle of creation began to take momentum when Gaia mated with Uranus and gave birth to twelve Titans, three Cyclops, and the three Hundred-Handed giants. Terrified by his six horrific children, Uranus trapped them within their uncle; Tartarus. Mother Gaia felt deep pain for her imprisoned children and wanted to avenge them, while Cronus, the youngest of the Titans, felt intimidated by his father's power. Seeing as he trapped his brothers in the underworld, he started feeling vulnerable. Which is why when Gaia instructed him to wound his father with a sickle of her creation, Cronus happily obliged. Yet, his mother didn't know of his ulterior motives.

A new age began for Gaia and Cronus when he wounded his father. Because from his blood, Gaia created Ash-tree nymph, three furies and giants, and Aphrodite. As for Cronus, he took his father's place and ruled over Heaven. However, Cronus wasn't very different from his father. Filled with hate and fear towards his monstrous brothers, he trapped them once again in their former cage.

Everything seemed to be perfect under his rule. The Meliae, better known as the Ast-tree nymphs, gave birth to the first humans, and Cronus married Rhea, his older sister. Life was wonderful until his parents warned him that he would suffer the same fate he had subjected his father to. The new king didn't accept the fact that one of his children might overthrow him, and so Cronus swallowed his children whole without remorse. Saddened by her husband's cruelty, Rhea tricked Cronus into eating a stone covered with a cloth instead of her youngest son, Zeus. She then sent her son to Crete, where he could grow up in secrecy. The nymphs took care of baby Zeus until he grew up and wanted to seek revenge. He sought help from Metis, his aunt. She fashioned an enchanted potion that would make Cronus vomit Zeus' siblings whole. Zeus disguised himself as a cupbearer to Cronus and deviously poured the potion in the wine without anyone knowing.

Shortly, after Cronus had drunk the wine, he felt a strong stomach ache and started vomiting his children one by one. Cronus had finally released Poseidon, Hades, Hera, Demeter, and Hestia. Zeus was happy to see his siblings well and alive, but he knew that his job wasn't over. He was clever enough to know that Gaia's six trapped children would aid him in the war against his father. Without a second thought, he traveled to the underworld and slew the first dragon and rushed to open the gates and release his uncles. Zeus took his uncles to live with him on Mount Olympus, where they plotted against the king and vowed to wage war on him. Grateful for Zeus' efforts, they gave him a lightning bolt that he could use in war. They also gave Poseidon a trident, and Hades a helmet that made him invisible.

Together, they were called the Olympians, and they fought against Cronus and the Titans led by Atlas. Naturally, the Olympians won the war, and Zeus cast the Titans away in Tartarus. Ironically, they were guarded by the Hundred-Headed giants, who were once in their place. He also decided to divide the universe between him and his brothers; Zeus ruled over Heaven, Hades governed the underworld, and Poseidon reigned over the oceans and seas.

The Origins of Medusa

Gaia didn't only have children with Uranus. She also had children with Pontus, a primordial sea god. Together, they gave birth to five Greek gods and goddesses. Two of their offspring, Phorcys, and Ceto, got married. Ceto was a beautiful sea goddess, who was also associated with sharks, whales, and other bloodcurdling sea monsters. Her husband wasn't that different from her either, except for the fact that he was more monstrous and frequently connoted with the dangers of the seas. According to Greek mythology, Phorcys was directly responsible for creating unspeakable sea monsters that terrified sailors who dared to sail in his sea. Unlike Ceto, Phorcys' body reflected his fearsome power; he had red skin, crab claws, and forelegs that spread out of his mermaid tail.

These two sea monsters were very prominent in Greek mythology because they were directly responsible for giving birth to every fearsome creature that terrified the hearts of mortals and caused chaos amidst the immortals. Among these were the three Gorgon sisters; Euryale, Stheno, and Medusa.

Here's where the mythology begins to divert. There's one version where the three gorgon sisters were beautiful monsters. Their hair strands were venomous snakes, and their eyes could turn any man to stone. The gorgons were feared creatures amongst the mortals. Another version of the story depicts Medusa as a beautiful maiden; so beautiful, in fact, that Poseidon grew fond of her and shamelessly took her and raped her in Athena's temple. Enraged by the heinous act that took place in her temple, Athena turned Medusa into a terrifying monster that no man dared to look directly at.

However, in both versions of the myth, Medusa is mortal, which is why Perseus was able to decapitate her and give her head to Polydectes, King of Seriphus, as per his request. After Medusa was murdered in her sleep, her blood had been spilled everywhere, and from it rose Pegasus and his brother Chrysaor, sons of Poseidon. Whether Medusa had fallen victim to the selfish acts of the gods, or she was, in fact, a deadly monster, she still played a prominent part in the mythology. In fact, people at the time sculpted her head on the walls to protect them from the evil eye.

The Weaves of Arachne

Deep in the heart of Greece, there was a young, fine maiden named Arachne. Arachne wasn't only beautiful, but she was also a very talented weaver. People, nymphs, and all kinds of creatures would stare at her beautifully woven pieces in awe. Because of her diverse audience, whispers about her work traveled fast until it reached Olympus. Arachne's talent didn't spark any god or goddesses' attention, except for Athena. Which was natural, given that Athena was the goddess of war and wisdom, and also had a gift for weaving.

Arachne's audience increased day after day, and so did her ego. The skillful young woman began bragging about her talent. She explained that she was so gifted to a point where not even Athena could compete against her. But, little did she know, Athena was listening to her claims. And, so the goddess decided to come down to Earth to see Arachne's work for herself. She disguised herself into an old woman and saw that Arachne's pieces were indeed beautiful. She then went to encourage and warn Arachne; the goddess told her that she was talented, but comparing her talent to a goddess was absolute foolishness. Arachne didn't heed Athena's warning and pursued to affirm her claims.

Athena couldn't stand the girl's arrogance, so she decided to challenge her. The goddess spent the day in the same room with Arachne; they both wove until it was night. After weaving for a whole day, Athena was ready to see Arachne's work. The goddess had woven a cloth that depicted the gods and goddesses blessing mankind from Mount Olympus, while Arachne's piece, which was more beautiful, had the gods falling down from the heavens and getting drunk.

Enraged by Arachne's audacity, she reached out her arm and began transforming Arachne's fair body into something heinous. Suddenly, the young girl's hair fell out, her ears and nose disappeared, she sprouted four legs, and her whole body shrank until she became a tiny spider.

Orpheus' Journey to the Underworld

Greek mythology is known for its battles, gods and goddesses, monsters, and mythical creatures. However, that is not all there is to it. It's also prominent for its passionate love stories, especially the tragic ones.

It was a happy day in ancient Greece because it was Orpheus and Eurydice's wedding day. Everyone knew of Orpheus; his melodies always infiltrated the city and brought joy to all the creatures. On their wedding day, the couple thought it would be wise to have the god of weddings, Hymen, bless their marriage. And, he did, but he also left them with an unfortunate omen. He warned them that nothing this perfect could last forever.

Time passed on their wedding day, and Eurydice was seen singing amidst the fields by an immoral shepherd. He couldn't resist her beauty. His desires were stronger than him, and so he chased her and tried to force himself onto her. Eurydice was terrified by the man's vulgarity and tried to escape, but as she was running, a snake bit her foot, and she died.

Orpheus couldn't believe his ears when he heard about his wife. He felt deep grief and sang songs that made the city and the gods mourn with him. It wasn't until his father. Apollo, the god of music, advised him to travel to the underworld so he could bargain for his wife's soul. The gods protected Orpheus as he sank deeper and deeper into the underworld. He was first met with Cerberus, the hellhound, but he charmed it with his melodies.

He then made his way to Hades, the god of the underworld, and his wife, Persephone. He requested to retrieve his wife's soul back, so he could place it in her dead body. But that wasn't enough for Hades. So, Orpheus decided to do what he did best; he expressed his feelings of great grief through his music and song. The divine couple was touched by his sadness, which made Hades grant him his wish. However, Hades had one condition. He told Orpheus that his wife's soul would follow him back to the surface of the Earth, but as they made their way up, he should not look behind him.

With a grateful heart, Orpheus accepted the god's condition and was on his way to the gate. It was a long way from the underworld to the surface, but Orpheus wasn't worried; he had gotten what he had asked for. He began his journey to the surface, and he could hear his wife's footsteps behind him, which relieved him. But, the more Orpheus approached the surface, the more her footsteps began to fade. Orpheus started growing weary, and he couldn't fight his instinct; he needed to know if his wife's soul was still behind him. Overcome by his weakness, Orpheus looked back. And, as soon as his eyes lay on her, she was immediately pulled back into the underworld. Orpheus tried to go back for her, but Hades would not allow him to proceed. Orpheus went back to the surface alone and died.

Chapter 7 - The Aztecs

The Five Suns

According to the Aztecs, our world was not the first one ever created. It is the fifth, and it was only the result of a series of acts of creation, followed by other acts of destruction. Ever since the birth of the two gods, Tezcatlipoca and Quetzalcoatl, the two middle sons of the creator god Ometeotl, they had been fighting over who would be the sun to rule over the world. These fights were thought to be why the world had been destroyed four times, as per the Aztec Sun Stone, before arriving at this age.

Tezcatlipoca was the ruler of the first movement or phase of creation, also known as the sun of Earth. He ruled over a race of giants who dominated the world. When Quetzalcoatl saw that, he decided to strike down his brother, and throw him in the ocean. As payback, the struck down god transformed into a jaguar, an animal closely tied with the Earth element, and ate the race he once ruled over.

The second sun shone on the world, soon after, with Quetzalcoatl as the ruler of second Earth. In his jealousy, Tezcatlipoca decided to overthrow his brother's rule. Mighty winds filled the sky, on his command, and carried off Quetzalcoatl and the race of humans he presided over. It was then said that these people turned to monkeys, and with that, the second sun was destroyed.

The first sun was the sun of the Earth, the second was the sun of the wind, and the third was the sun of rain. The third world was overseen by Tlaloc, the god of rain. However, it wasn't long before Quetzalcoatl sent down ashes and fire from the heavens and ended this world, turning all humans into turkeys.

Tlaloc's wife, Chalchiuhtlicu, ruled over the sun of water. She was the goddess of waters, rivers, and seas, but her rule ended when a great flood came over the world and washed all creation away. The people had turned to fish, and the mountains were uprooted from the Earth. Aztec codices then differ on whether or not Tezcatlipoca had managed to save a man and his wife from the flood and tell them to hide away until the waters no longer covered the Earth.

Nevertheless, the only significance of this part is the resemblance it holds to Sumerian, Hebrew, and Christian texts, since one of the survivors eventually disobeyed Tezcatlipoca and started a fire, and for that, they were all killed.

With the four suns dying and the world destroyed, the gods were displeased. Instead of fighting, they allied to repair the Earth and the heavens. They created mankind to populate the Earth and maize for them as sustenance. Yet, the world was dark without a sun and a ruler. For that, the gods came together to decide on who was to be chosen, since, for the Aztecs, to create something, another must be sacrificed. Tecuciztecatl volunteered, but the gods nominated someone less prideful; they chose Nanahuatzin. Despite being full of sores and not as mighty as his contender, Nanahuatzin graciously accepted the duty.

The gods built two pyramids, the Pyramids of the Sun and Moon (still standing to this day), for the gods to fast and to present offerings before sacrificing themselves for the honor of becoming the sun. As they performed their rites, a sacrificial pyre burnt until it was hot enough for the gods to jump into the fire. Tecuciztecatl went first, yet backed down as he was hit by the flames. Nanahuatzin, then without hesitation, ran into the flames where his body burned to ashes. Following that, fueled by his own pride, Tecuciztecatl jumped into the flames right after seeing Nanahuatzin perform the feat he couldn't.

All around the gods, the world began to light up; the fifth sunrise was upon them. Nanahuatzin returned in a form so glorious that no one could look at him. He called himself Tonatiuh, Sun God. Minutes later, Tecuciztecatl also emerged as a bright sun, which worried the gods. Fearing that two suns would cause an imbalance, one god threw a rabbit at Tecuciztecatl in an attempt to take him down. Instead, he was wounded, which caused him to shine less brightly, and so he became the moon.

Another problem then arose. The celestial objects didn't move across the sky. Tonatiuh had become arrogant, and he demanded that the other gods sacrifice themselves to him if he was to move. Eventually, they agreed. Quetzalcoatl, being one of the high gods, took a sacrificial blade and cut out the hearts of all the other gods, thus setting the sun in motion, and with it the moon.

If you hadn't already guessed, this is the origins of the belief that human sacrifices were needed to keep the sun moving along its path and the world from collapsing.

New Capital

It wasn't easy for the Aztecs to find a home; they never found the right place to settle simply because the gods never approved.

The Aztecs originally lived in Aztlán; hence the name. However, Huitzilopochtli, the god of war, didn't approve of their way of living and instructed them to leave at once. He ordered them to abandon their name and refer to themselves as the "Mexica." The Aztecs were lost, and they didn't know where else to go, so Huitzilopochtli guided them at first until he instructed his sister, Malinalxochitl, goddess of the desert's reptiles, to guide them to their new land instead.

All was going well until Malinalxochitl started practicing witchcraft around them. The goddess had been summoning unwanted spirits to guide them to their new home. However, the Aztecs were highly uncomfortable and decided to summon Huitzilopochtli, so he could guide them once again.

Disappointed by her inadequacy, Huitzilopochtli put her into a deep sleep and ordered his people to leave the place they were in. His worshippers quickly obliged, fleeing the new home and covering their trail so that Malinalxochitl would not find them.

Sometime later, the goddess found herself stranded on her own. She quickly figured out what had happened and vowed to take revenge on her brother. Years passed and Malinalxochitl's son, Copil had grown up and desired to avenge his mother. Copil searched for the Aztecs along with their guide. Blinded by revenge, he underestimated his uncle and attempted to kill him, but Huitzilopochtli was a much better fighter than Copil ever was. Without hesitation, Huitzilopochtli reached into the boy's chest and ripped his heart out, then threw it into the lake.

After several decades, Huitzilopochtli ordered them to find the boy's heart in the lake and build their home on it. He told them they would find a long, prickly Cactus with an eagle on it eating a serpent. The Aztecs traveled long and far until they found the cactus that their god had described.

After many years of traveling, the Aztecs finally found a home upon an island in the Lago Texcoco.

Chapter 8 - Celtic Myths

Despite their religion and mythology crumbling against the Roman invasion, we still have several detailed accounts of their legendary tales. Granted, Celtic information preservation techniques were a lot more advanced in comparison to those known by ancient Sumerians. But, you'll see for yourself that the determining factor was the powerful emotions deep-seated within their epics.

Táin Bó Cúailnge | The Cattle Raid of Cooley

As the legend goes, Queen Medb had struck a deal with Dáire mac Fiachna, an Ulster cattle-lord, to rent his stud bull Donn Cuailnge. The bull was highly fertile, which made it a valuable asset that the queen needed to settle a dispute with her husband, Ailill. As a woman, she was ambitious, prideful, and strong of character; she didn't take well to defeat. So, when she realized her husband was richer than her by one bull, she set out to purchase a superior stud.

After agreeing to lend Medb his bull, Dáire overheard one of Medb's drunken messengers bellowing about how Queen Medb would have taken the bull by force if the man hadn't agreed to the trade willingly. With this shattering blow to his pride, Dáire backed down from the deal, which angered Medb.

The warrior queen didn't take long to assemble her army, and with her husband's aid, as well as a group of Ulster-exiles led by Ulster's dethroned king, Fergus mac Roich, Medb's army marched to Ulster. When she got there, the men of Ulster fell to their knees in agony because of a curse set on them by their own patron goddess, Macha. She had plagued the men of

Ulster with a curse that sent them to the ground with blinding pain for four days and five nights. Because one Ulster king forced her to race against his horses while she was pregnant with twins, the curse was made to take effect during times of war, when they most needed their strength.

When Queen Medb saw the men writhing on the ground, she knew it was her chance to steal the bull. But, while all the men were incapacitated, there was one seventeen-year-old boy, Cú Chulainn, who leaped to defend his people - his age had kept him protected from the curse. Cú Chulainn was characterized with great strength and fighting skills ever since he was a child, and was prophesied to become one of the great heroes of his time. With the help of his companion and charioteer, Láeg, he started hacking at Medb's army little by little while riding away on his chariot. Finally, he managed to cease the fight by invoking the right of single combat.

Given his looks, the queen did not think much of the boy and agreed to let him defend his people based on the terms of single combat. Duel after duel, the boy kept winning. Cú Chulainn was killing off Med's army soldier by soldier. He was stuck in an endless series of one-on-one battles, and despite holding back the army, he wasn't able to stop the queen from taking Donn Cuailnge, the stud bull, to herself.

Looking upon the boy's situation and delighting in watching men fight, Morrigan, the Irish goddess of battle, chose to interfere. She came to his tent in the form of a woman, offering to bed him. However, when he rebuked her and denied her favors, she turned vengeful. She revealed her true form and vowed to hinder him in his fights to come.

Morrigan used her shape-shifting abilities to interfere with the boy's fight. She transformed herself into a cow and charged at him as he was fighting Loch mac Mofebis. Then, she took the form of an eel and swam in the shallow waters in which they were fighting. In retaliation, he took a slash at her and wounded her. After that, she turned into a wolf and attacked him, which allowed his opponent to sink his blade deep into the boy's flesh. This triggered one of Cú Chulainn's famous ríastrad episodes in which he mutated into a powerful humanoid creature and hacked, slashed and sliced maniacally with his trident, the Gáe Bulg. Needless to say, he defeated his opponent instantly and was left alone by the goddess.

As he fought, he grew weary, and after one fight in which he had sustained serious injuries, he was spent. During the night, while resting and looking hopelessly upon the horde of warriors he still had yet to fight, he saw a tall warrior clad in a silk tunic walking toward him, clasping a shield and two spears in his hands. The divine-looking man identified himself as the boy's real father, Lugh, the god of light. He comforted the boy, spoke to him kindly, then healed his wounds, and sent him into a deep sleep for three days. Meanwhile, the god took Cú Chulainn's place, fighting off enemies, as the boy recovered.

During these three days, while the men of Ulster were still under Macha's curse, and while their hero was put to sleep, the youth battalion of Emain Macha (the capital province of Ulster) had heard of what was happening to Cú Chulainn and leaped to his aid. These one hundred and fifty boys, all the same age as Cú Chulainn or even less, were heavily trained from the moment they were able to wield a sword. However, despite their skills and passion, they were outmanned by Medb's army, and that led to their demise.

The battle between the youth battalion and the queen's army ended in a bloody massacre in which none of the boys escaped. When Cú Chulainn woke up, he saw what had become of the boys he once knew and trained with as a child, and was overcome with another fit of unquenchable rage. The massacre had triggered his battle frenzy; his ríastrad. The boy, now looking like a gruesome monster, picked up his trident and hopped upon his chariot. He drove through his enemies' camp, killing and slaying everyone.

Armed with supernatural strength and speed, and driven by his anger, it is said that Cú Chulainn had killed so many men that their piled-up bodies had begun to look like a wall more than a pile. He killed one-hundred and thirty soldiers that day, in addition to the other casualties he caused. But, even then, Medb still had powerful opponents prepared for him to face. First, she had him face Calatin, a wizard, his twenty-seven sons, and their poisoned spear-tips.

When he emerged victoriously, she forced Cú Chulainn's dear friend, Ferdia, to go against him. The fight went on from morning until the sun was in the middle of the sky without bloodshed. Then, Ferdia regretfully drew first blood and was followed by Cú Chulainn's swift reprisal, which led to Ferdia's death. Cú Chulainn fell to his knees in exhaustion and despair. He had just killed a man he had considered a brother and was severely injured, as well.

Medb's army took that as a sign to charge the walls of Ulster, but by then, the curse had worn off. The men of Ulster were ready for battle, and so they did, with Cú Chulainn by their side. Finally, the hero found himself facing Medb, but spared her life, for he refused to kill a woman. With that, Ulster won the battle, and peace between them and the warrior queen. As for the bull, he had escaped from Medb amidst all the fighting and went off to fight Ailill's bull. He ended up winning but got himself injured in the process, and he eventually died. With that, the epic ended.

Deirdre of the Sorrows

This is the tale of Deirdre, a woman of indescribable beauty, and how one prophesy took her down a path of misery. The events of this tragic story take place in the time when Fergus mac Roich was still in the service of Ulster.

In a time of peace, Ulster king, Conchobar mac Nessa, went to attend a great feast in his honor prepared by Fedlimid mac Daill - accounts differ on whether he was the king's bard or one of Ulster's lords. Among other people, in his company were the druid Cathbad and the king's right-hand, Fergus mac Roich. Wine was brought in from Greece and meat was roasted, and the men were eating and drinking to their hearts' content when the feast was interrupted by a messenger.

Fedlimid received news that he had become a father to a daughter. In celebration, the king told Cathbad to look into the girl's future and tell them what his druid eyes see. Her horoscope foretold an unsettling story. While the girl was to grow up a fair maiden, "fairest among the women of Erin," she would be the cause of a great loss for Ulster; many men would go to war over her. Those loyal to their province, of which there were many, asked Fedlimid to kill her for Ulster's sake, but the king demanded silence.

Stirred by Cathbad's description, he told Fedlimid that he'd have the daughter sent away and cared for by Levarcam, a wise elderly woman. Then, when she had become of age, the king would take her to himself, saving Ulster from any potential danger. Fedlimid agreed and, before sending her away, he named her Deirdre, which stood for, "broken-hearted."

The girl grew up to be as beautiful as Cathbad had prophesized, and as per the king's commandments, she was only allowed to see Levarcam, Cathbad, and the king himself. But, as time passed, Deirdre grew to realize that she didn't love Conchobar. One day, as she sat with Levarcam looking over the snow-covered woods, she spoke about the man of her dreams. He would have hair as black as a raven, skin as white as snow, and cheeks as red as blood, she said. Her caretaker knew who she was looking for, and she told her of whom she was dreaming; it was Naoise mac Uisneach, a knight of the Red Branch, the king's house.

After Deidre's begging and pleading, and out of love, Levarcam brought Naoise to speak with her. After seeing the young man, the thought of being wedded to the king loomed over her life like a dark cloud. And, while her beauty captivated Naoise, he couldn't take her away from the king. But he couldn't resist her for long. He went back to seek the help of his brothers and returned one night again to save his love.

Along with Naoise's brethren, Ardan and Ainnle, the two lovers fled to Scotland by sea. After living among the people there for a while, they had to run away again because the Scottish king also had eyes for fair Deidre. Finally, they settled in Glen Etive where they lived in isolation, sustaining themselves. But that is not where the story ends.

Once Conchobar was told of what had happened, he held back his rage. Instead of sending his soldiers after them, he waited.

Years later, he sent Fergus to offer them a safe return to Ulster, and to tell them that the king has forgiven and forgotten. Gladly, all but Deidre agreed. She smelled a whiff of evil in the air but went along after being blamed for her distrust in the king and in Fergus' protection.

On the way back, Fergus was met by a friend who invited him to stay the night. Despite wanting to deliver his company safely to Ulster, he was bound by a geas (an obligation that could bring doom and misfortune if violated), so he had to stay and have his sons escort the estranged party back home. At last, they arrived safely at the House of the Red Branch where they were warmly welcomed, but not by the king.

Instead of rushing to receive them, Conchobar sent for Levercam. He wanted to know what the years had done to Deidre's beauty. The old woman claimed that the wild had run its course to save Deidre from him, but her lie did not hold up for long. The king had sent spies who spoke of nothing but the woman's fairness.

With that, Conchobar took his men and went to seize Deidre. He ordered his men to kill Fergus' sons and had Cathbad cast a spell that entrapped the rest of the party in slime. Naoise and his brothers were captured and slain by Owen mac Duracht. After that, the king had Deidre for himself, but towards him, she was colder than winter.

Angry and resentful, Conchobar asked her what she hated most in the world, and she replied with the name of the man who decapitated Naoise. He then told her she was going to be sent to stay at Owen's house for a year. Surrounded by her oppressors, she refused to look them in the eye as she went on the chariot. When Conchobar noticed, he exclaimed mockingly, "Deirdre, the glance of thee between me and Owen is the glance of a ewe between two rams." As if in rebellion, Deidre jumped off the wagon, head first onto a rock, and died.

Within the two stories, one could notice that Celtic myths were quite different from those of other cultures. While some, like the Greeks and the Sumerians, had prominent sexual themes, the Celts' tales revolved around emotion, tragedy, and honor. But, keep in mind, this doesn't mean that the cultures did not overlap in some ways.

Conclusion

The quote, "History repeats itself," isn't just a cautionary statement that has ironically been repeated by multiple authors. Repetition isn't a trick from the universe or a punishment from the gods. When it comes down to it, it's the innate human behavior that leads to an expected ending to all of our stories.

History can seem like it's made up of countless ancient and modern stories, but when taking a deeper look at it, we find that it's simply one story told by several people from different times.

Every mythology nearly starts out the same way; "In the beginning, there was chaos." Chaos didn't necessarily mean that the world was in disarray. It just meant that one element had dominated the universe, and there was nothing else but it.

In Sumerian mythology, there was nothing except for the primordial sea. This sentence should sound familiar because this exact description was also found in Egyptian mythology. However, chaos wasn't always water. It took on different forms in other mythologies. In Chinese mythology, for instance, chaos was depicted as an overwhelming element that had been dominating the universe until it folded onto itself and created a cosmic egg. This idea was also reinforced in Greek mythology, except chaos created Gaia and not an egg. However, there was a cosmic egg that was produced amidst chaos in Egyptian mythology.

Chaos wasn't the only common element between these mythologies. They also had similar gods and goddesses. Aztec mythology has the god, Ometeotl, who was both male and female. Ometeotl represented duality in their culture. History documents the same idea three centuries later in the Dahomean mythology, where the god of the sun and the moon were one. Even though they were independent entities, they were referred to as one being called Mawu. And, together they represented duality in the West African Culture.

Dahomean mythology also has other common elements. For instance, it depicts an ancient serpent who carries the Earth. His name is Ayida-Weddo. History records that same creature in the Aboriginal's mythology. To them, this ancient serpent is the ultimate creator.

There are countless common elements that could be found between numerous mythologies, but there is one truth that they all contain: The Magic and Power of stories. Whether it was to explain the world around them, or to make sense of occurrences out of their hands, people always turned to story-telling. And it is these stories, and the lessons we learn from them, that have lived through the centuries, and will continue to do so for so much more.